D1050926

# MONSTERS

## Monsters in a Mess

DISCARDED

## by Candice Ransom
## illustrated by Tyrell Solomon

Ready-to-Read

Simon Spotlight

New York   London   Toronto   Sydney   New Delhi

To Audrey, Claire, and Priya –C. R.

To my mom, Tiffany, and

my brother, Tyree –T. S.

SIMON SPOTLIGHT
An imprint of Simon & Schuster Children's Publishing Division
1230 Avenue of the Americas, New York, New York 10020
This Simon Spotlight edition August 2022
Text copyright © 2022 by Candice Ransom
Illustrations copyright © 2022 by Tyrell Solomon
For information about special discounts for bulk purchases, please contact Simon &
Schuster Special Sales at 1-866-506-1949 or business@simonandschuster.com.
Manufactured in the United States of America 0722 LAK
2 4 6 8 10 9 7 5 3 1
Library of Congress Cataloging-in-Publication Data
Names: Ransom, Candice F., 1952– author. | Solomon, Tyrell, illustrator. Title: Monsters in
a mess / by Candice Ransom ; illustrated by Tyrell Solomon. Description: New York :
Simon Spotlight, 2022. | Series: Red truck monsters | Summary: "A family of
monsters clean their messy house to make space for their new pet goldfish"— Provided by
publisher. Identifiers: LCCN 2021043650 (print) | LCCN 2021043651 (ebook) |
ISBN 9781665901703 (paperback) | ISBN 9781665901710 (hardcover) |
ISBN 9781665901727 (ebook) Subjects: CYAC: Stories in rhyme. | Monsters—Fiction. |
Trucks—Fiction. | Pets—Fiction. | Goldfish—Fiction. | House cleaning—Fiction. |
LCGFT: Stories in rhyme. | Picture books. Classification: LCC PZ8.3.R1467 Mo 2022
(print) | LCC PZ8.3.R1467 (ebook) | DDC [E]—dc23
LC record available at https://lccn.loc.gov/2021043650
LC ebook record available at https://lccn.loc.gov/2021043651

Red truck monsters
off to shop.
Parents, kids,
down they hop.

Monsters take
a morning stroll,
buy a goldfish
in a bowl.

"Henry?"

"Jane?"

"Its name is Bill."

Red truck motors up
the hill.

Once at home
they look around.

Not an empty spot
is found!

Is there space
for little Bill?
No room
on the windowsill.

Bathtubs here
and flat tires there.
Junk and clutter
everywhere.

Dishes, puppets,
socks, and such.
Mama monster cries,
"Too much!"

"We must clean up.
Move those sleds.
Clear out closets,
under beds."

Monsters sweat
and monsters stress.
Monsters tackle
great big mess.

Tractors, trucks,
and building blocks.
Busted clocks that
lost their tocks.

Keep on clearing!
Pitch! Toss! Squish!
Still no place
for one small fish.

Out goes garbage.
Out goes trash.
Say goodbye
to fake mustache.

Donate goods that others can use. Pictures, soup pots, new tap shoes.

Boxes all go
in the back.
Will they all fit?
Push! Squeeze! Stack!

Dump is busy
as a fair.
Recycle here.
Donate there.

Back at home
the family beams.
Floor to ceiling,
their house gleams!

# No junk or clutter anywhere.

But . . . Bill's bowl
seems kind of bare.

Monsters take
another spin.

Bill comes along.
See Bill grin!

Twisty highway.

Water slops.

"Hey! A yard sale!"
Red truck stops.

# Smart idea?

# Not a bit.

Fishy lampshades!
Goldfish game!
Painting kit
to paint Bill's name!

Pirate, mermaid.
Buy! Buy! Buy!
Stuff in red truck
hits the sky!

Also . . .

Castle, seaweed,
treasure chest.
Bill the fish
gets all the best!

Monsters call it
Mess Sweet Mess.